TREATMENT

BY

RALPH H. PERKINS

This book is a work of fiction.
Names, characters, places, and incidents are
the product of the author's imagination or are
used fictitiously. Any resemblance to actual events,
locales, or persons, living or dead, is coincidental.

ISBN: 0615686605
ISBN-13: 9780615686608

Library of Congress Control Number: 2012915379
Ralph Perkins Publishing, Sunny Isles Beach, Florida

For my children,
You give me the strength to carry-on.

INTRODUCTION

In 2008 and 2009, the unemployment rate averaged at around ten percent, and the country was in a Great Recession. California was one of the states hit very hard by this recession, and all of its funds were depleted. In an effort to increase the state revenue, the governor of the state issued a base sales tax increase from 7.25 percent to 8.25 percent, and some cities and counties added additional taxes, which raised sales tax rates to above ten percent. Personal state income taxes were increased by 0.25 percent, dependent tax credits were *reduced* by $210 for each dependent, and registration and annual vehicle licensing fees doubled.[1] Some say there was another private meeting held with state law enforcement officials, and discussions in this meeting were then pushed down to local law enforcement agencies. Local agencies explained that police officers needed to crack down and write more tickets and issue more arrests so that the state and local counties could collect additional revenue and state employees could keep their current jobs. Some of these tickets and arrests may not have been warranted.

---

[1] (State of California)
State of California. (n.d.). *State of California Franchise Tax Board*. Retrieved 2009, from CA.gov: www.ftb.ca.gov

CHAPTER ONE

IT IS a dark, rainy night, with thunder roaring in the distance. A man holds a gun to the temple of another man as the man's family looks on. The cathedral-size windows in the house rattle with each thunderstrike. As the gunman looks around the room, he sees happy pictures of the victim and his family, including his son's baseball photo and several family holiday photos all along the wall. The wielding gunman also notices an officer's badge and an award for outstanding police service. He looks back at the man, who is now on his knees sweating and begging for his family's life and his own. As the thunder strikes again, the gunman's mind drifts back as he considers how he got here and why he is doing this.

FEBRUARY 2008

It is a sunny morning in Miami, Florida, as Richard takes a shower in his house. As the water shoots down on his head, he hears his wife Mary yelling out to him in the background.

"Richard, are you listening to me?" she asks. "You need to make sure you are home early today to pick the kids up at school before you leave for California."

Richard smiles, opens the glass door, and leaps out of the shower soaking wet. He has a huge smile on his face as he agrees to Mary's request and gives her a kiss on the forehead.

He is just about dressed as two adorable kids come running in, an eleven-year-old boy and his six-year-old sister. "Daddy, Daddy, Daddy!" the girl yells. "Are you going to pick us up after school today before you go to California?"

"Of course," Richard says as he hugs her and gives a fist bump to his son. "Umm, little Richie and Jenny, I think someone left toys in daddy's bedroom last night when we were playing superheroes. Let's go guys. Pick up the capes and guns before the evil bank robber comes looking for you little superheroes. Ha ha ha!"

"Daddy," Jenny says, "do you think mommy will play with us next time?"

"Yeah, she never plays," says little Richie.

Richard is a loving father, maybe because his parents have been dead for over nine years and he misses their time together.

His parents died as a result of a car accident while they were on vacation in North Carolina. Richard, who was extremely close to both of them, still harbors some pain over the matter. His parents were driving in icy weather, and the local county employees never got around to de-icing the road, so their 2000 Honda Accord spun out on the ice, slamming into an SUV that was stalled on the highway and killing both of them instantaneously.

While still getting ready for work, Richard clicks on the flat-screen television mounted on the bedroom wall. The local news station reports record layoffs. The news mentions the collapse of AIG and the American auto industry before going into detail about the Bernie Madoff Ponzi scheme and some of Madoff's victims like Richard's boss, Mr. Smothers.

The anchor reports, "...and one of Miami's very own, local millionaire ad tycoon Alan Smothers. Smothers's loss is unreported, but we estimate it to be no less than three million dollars. Smothers's Ad Group has been hurting as well and just had a record layoff of about three hundred employees, including some top executives. More layoffs are expected here in Miami at Smothers's Ad Group and at their other locations across the United States. In other news, the state of California is out of money. In a speech by Governor Schwarzenegger, the governor says that he will do whatever it takes to get the state back on track. Up next, will the housing and auto industry ever bounce back?"

Mary comes in and turns off the television. "Stop watching all this bad news. You're lucky you still have your job," she says.

Richard answers with a sexy grin. "Baby, Smothers needs me. I'll be fine."

"Well, don't give them any reason."

Richard stops her mid-sentence. "Stop worrying. I'll be fine. I *own* these guys. Besides, at the rate you're spending our money I'll have to get a second job or refinance the house again to pay off the credit card debit you're racking up. The one damn job you had, you spent more money working there than your customers did. I mean, really, Jenny is now six years old and you had promised that you would go back to work fulltime and help pay off our enormous debt you helped create. It seems like we are always arguing about this and nothing changes"

"Listen Rich, I'll go back soon, but you know I have the girls' weekend coming up, and Jenny gets out of school at two o'clock, so I can really only work for a few hours. It really doesn't make much sense to go back yet," whines Mary.

Richard replies a little more stern, "I'm not sure if you understand what is happening right now with the economy, even though I tried explaining to you hundred times. But we are in for some tough times. Are you really listening to the news? Record lay-offs, banks are taking huge loses, and the housing market is going to shit. It's getting tough out there. And I have been telling you for almost a year now to stop spending. But no, you still go to the fucking salon every week with your girlfriends and get hair, nails, and god knows what else done."

"But I like to look good for you. Do you like the way I look?" asks Mary.

"Yeah, you look great, but you would still look great even if you didn't go with those girls to the salon once a week and throw money around like it was free. Then, to top it off, did you listen to me about not spending at the mall? Noooo, you didn't. You still buy something in the mall every day. It's like shopping is your job," argues Rich.

At a higher volume Mary says, "You travel all the time and leave me here stuck by myself. All I have are those girls, our shopping trips together, and our salon days. I'm neglected Rich," says Mary, now almost in tears.

"Oh stop, you have a big house, fancy cars, a personal trainer, a spare bedroom that is your personal closet," states Rich. Now with a smile on his face, "Also, when I'm in town, don't you get a chance to go out twice a week with your girlfriends to clubs and bars?"

Mary, with her head hanging low, nods and with a whisper so low Rich can't hear says, "It's not the money. It's the time."

As he leaves for work, Richard kisses Mary and his children good-bye. They live in a nice-size home, and Richard brings in an above average living. Little Richy plays sports, and Jenny attends dance school. They are also prominent members of their local church congregation.

However, as soon as the kids go to school and Richard leaves for work, which is often out of state, Mary meets her lover, who is also her personal trainer. Despite her perfect, white picket fence suburbia life and the fact that she is still in love with her husband, Mary believes her lover gives her the excitement that she feels her marriage is missing. Much younger than she is, Mary's trainer makes her feel youthful again. *If only Richard knew*, she thought, *he wouldn't be paying for these personal training sessions anymore.*

CHAPTER TWO

A LOUD boom is heard as thunder strikes again. Richard stands in the police officer's living room. Richard yelling and kicking the officer, keeps repeating, "I had a life. I had a life." As Richard almost starts to cry, Rich says, "I had a life."

The thunder roars again and Richard has a flashback to a meeting room, where he is pitching an automobile manufacturer on why the ad agency of Smothers and Smothers, for which he is the very young-looking thirty-four-year-old vice president, is the best ad agency for them. As the meeting progresses, the gentlemen from the automobile manufacturer laugh and congratulate Richard on his creativity. He remembers one man saying

"Sounds good. We'll see you in Sacramento tomorrow."
Richard remembers giving a huge smile and shaking his
head, agreeing that he'll be there. Then he remembers
Mr. Smothers, a man in his mid-to-late fifties, walking
up after the meeting saying, "My boy, you're flying this
solo out there in California."

After picking up the kids after school and then eating dinner with his family, Richard grabs his packed
bag and heads for the airport. Once there, he goes
through security and then waits patiently at his gate,
reviewing his advertising proposal for his meeting in
California.

On the plane, Richard is very social. In between flip-
ping papers and studying his notes, he speaks to both
passengers sitting next to him. The passengers in front
of and behind him turn their heads trying to listen in
too, wishing they were part of the conversation. Due to
his keen sense for marketing and advertising, Richard
points out the irony of the sale in the *Sky Magazine* that
he took from the pocket of the seat in front of him. On
one page they are advertising a self-breathalyzer test,
and on the adjacent page they are advertising wine,
wine chillers, beer taps, and cases to conceal alcohol,
like flasks and flask binoculars.

"I swear, what marketing geniuses these *Sky Magazine* people are," Richard says. "Buy it, hide it, and then test yourself before you drive."

His keen sense of marketing shines again when Richard describes the sales presentation of the flight attendant as she tries to sell all the passengers headphones, snacks, food, and alcoholic beverages. Richard buys none of these and pulls out his Prada briefcase instead. Inside the briefcase he pulls out his own set of headphones that look a lot nicer than the five-dollar ones the flight attendants were hocking moments earlier. Richard also grabs a packed bag of peanuts—no free airline nuts for him. As the other passengers fall asleep during the six-hour plane ride, Richard works, studying his presentation notes. When the plane finally lands, he walks off and is immediately greeted by one of his company's local ad guys, Kevin Garrison. They shake hands and give each other a friendly man hug. Richard and Kevin both reach out their right hands and while shaking hands they hug one another chest high with only the upper part of their bodies touching one another.

"What up big man!" says Kevin.

"Nothing much, my brother," Rich replies.

Both men acknowledge that it's great to see each other again and start reminiscing about the times they spent hanging out when Kevin worked in Atlanta and Richard was the lead on the Coca-Cola advertising project.

Richard remembers a particular noisy after-party when he and Kevin were drinking and doing shots to celebrate nailing the Coca-Cola account. Kevin was yelling with a little slur in his voice, "I fucking love this guy," while wearing a blinking red Coca-Cola button. "Doesn't everyone fucking love this guy?" Kevin asked their fellow business associates. The group of fifty businessmen and women all yelled in unison, "Yes!" Then, Mr. Smothers got up as the head of the party and everyone immediately quieted down. Smothers said with a very serious look on his face, "I just have one thing to say about Richard Park. Today, Richard...I fucking love you too." The whole place immediately went into an uproar with everyone yelling, "Rich, Rich, Rich, Rich, Rich, Rich, Rich, Rich," with Kevin yelling the loudest. Richard stood with a huge smile on his face while everyone is chanting.

"So Rich, Rich, Rich," Kevin says as he and Richard drive away from the airport.

"Ooh, what did you say?" Richard replies hesitantly. "Sorry, Kev, I'm kind of out of it a little."

"Long flight, huh? I just wanted to know what our strategy is on this Honda deal, big guy. I'm sure you have something smooth up your sleeve."

"Oh yeah, baby, I got something planned," Richard replies, a sly grin on his face. "Hey, nice job on landing that executive jet airliner company, by the way."

"Yeah, there was nothing to it, my man. You know I learned from the best," Kevin says, laughing.

CHAPTER THREE

AS RICH starts to talk to Kevin, a crash of lighting flickers outside the car. Richard stands in the officer's living room with the gun in his hand as a terrible storm is bearing down outside through the cathedral windows. He is now sweating as much as the officer and his family are. The officer's wife is now tied up with duct tape over her mouth as she clutches her children, and the police officer's hands are bound behind his back with his own handcuffs.

"How do those handcuffs feel, Officer?" Richard asks condescendingly. "They aren't pinching your skin at the wrists, are they?"

Richard kicks the officer in the stomach. The officer's wife and children wince from the blow as if they were being kicked as well. The officer, who is now gagged, bellies over and chokes a little. A small amount of blood drips out of his nose when he breathes through it. Richard begins to walk around the room almost, as if he's presenting to a board of directors as he's done so many times in the past when pitching marketing ideas.

"Well, I hope you've enjoyed your life these last six months, officer. Oh yeah, because I sure have." Richard has a nasty grin on his face and laughs a psychotic, condescending laugh. "You got a real nice family here. Wife, two kids, nice big house with a white picket fence just like I had," he says. "Ooh, look," Richard remarks as he glances over to a set of keys lying on the officer's coffee table. "I see you even own a fucking Honda. Perfect, just fucking perfect," Richard says, almost sounding defeated. "Let me tell you a little story about Honda," Richard says while bending down to the officer's wife, who is crying uncontrollably and clutching both children, looking at Richard as if he is a monster. "You think I'm a monster, *Right?*" yells Richard. He's right. He is a monster who has no fear, no mercy, no remorse, no life, and nothing to lose. Lightning crashes once again.

"Mr. Park, so why do you think this strategy will work for Honda?" says a white-haired man in a very expensive-looking suit.

"Well, Mr. Collin, you see, with everything we laid out here and the focus of your competition of cutting ad spending, we are in fact raising it," says Richard.

"Yes, Mr. Park, I understand that, but *Why*" Mr. Collin asks in a loud, overpowering voice.

"Well, I want every person who is considering buying a new car to not just buy any vehicle. I want them to buy a Honda," Richard says. "And they will want to buy a Honda because we are going to own every goddamned market with radio, TV, Internet, newspapers, magazines, letters, and anything else we can throw at them. Honda will be the first manufacturer every consumer comes to for a vehicle. People are still buying cars. There may not be a lot of people still buying cars in this downturned market, but some are still buying. With all media being sold for dirt cheap, it's a no-brainer. Now, would you rather stop by General Motors first because they feel bad that the American auto market is dying and GM is boasting 'Buy American?'" Richard asks aggressively.

Mr. Collin attempts to slide in a statement, "But—"

Richard immediately shuts him down. "I know you employ just as many, if not more, Americans than GM does. So don't you have the right to say that to the whole country? 'Honda employs just as many Americans as GM does. We have factory plants in the US, and we are here to stay.' Honda will be the first place to shop for a new vehicle." Richard shows his cocky smile to Mr. Collin and the entire Honda board, which consists of about fifteen members, both men and women, who all wait with anticipation to see what will be said next.

Richard takes a seat at the head of the conference table in the big glass conference room, a giant Honda logo in light blue neon light behind him. He looks over at Mr. Collin, who is shaking his head in agreement and smiling back at him.

Richard's grin turns to stone, however, as he gazes across the table at the Honda logo residing on Mr. Collin's coffee mug, thinking back on the time when he stood in the snow at the impound lot in North Carolina as his parents' smashed 2000 Honda Accord was being reviewed by a local police officer for any valuables that Richard might want. A cold blank stare was on Richard's bundled, freezing face. However, despite it being so cold, Richard looked almost catatonic as the local North Carolina police officer spoke to him about wanting any of his parents' belongings, including their vacation bags, which had been pulled from the trunk of their car. Richard had no response and just kept staring straight ahead.

"Wow, that was awesome. You had old Dick Collin eating out of your hand," Kevin says loudly.

He and Richard are sitting in a local trendy bar in Sacramento. Richard has a cold, blank stare on his face. The bar looks like something Richard would usually see in a trendy city, such as New York or Philly, and not in Sacramento, California. The bar is narrow, with brick alongside the walls. On one side of the room is a long, narrow wood bar, which makes the place look like an alleyway. The bar has metal barstools with black leather seat surfaces that sit atop a smooth black floor. Overhead are glowing neon lights attached to spinning shiny metal fan blades, each fan a different color. Below the pink glowing neon fan between the front entrance and the bar is a fat female DJ spinning CDs. There is very little space to dance on what appears to be the dance floor in front of her, but it doesn't matter, since no one is dancing anyway. It's about ten o'clock and the bar is kind of slow, with only about fifteen people there, including Kevin and Richard.

"Yeah, it was kind of great wasn't it, Kevin, my man," Richard says with a big smile.

"Old Man Smothers is going to love you, man," Kevin says admiringly. "This Honda deal could really save the company."

"Okay, bro, enough talk about shop," Richard says. "Let's do a shot, but first I need to call my wife and kids and wish them a good night before they go to sleep. Remember, they are three hours ahead of us."

One shot down and Richard orders a Captain Morgan and Diet Coke.

"Give me the same, but I need real Coke, not that diet shit that this guy is drinking," Kevin says to the bartender.

They order two more drinks and the place begins hopping as more people walk in. Richard walks outside and calls home to speak to Mary and the kids. He speaks to both little Richy and Jenny separately, who were about to go to bed, and wishes them a good night. They were both up late watching a movie. Richard then speaks to Mary.

"What are you doing now? Did you land the Honda deal?" she asks.

Richard replays the scene in the conference room in his mind. "Absolutely I did. This deal is going to be huge, and maybe it will even make me a real partner," he says. "Kevin and I are out at some local bar having some drinks now to celebrate.""That's wonderful, honey," she says, a sense of excitement in her voice. "So does that mean I can renew my personal training classes for another six months?"

"Let's go, Rich! I got some shots waiting," Kevin yells out to Richard.

"Listen, honey, I gotta run," Richard says to Mary. "I'll talk to you tomorrow night when I get home. Love you. Bye."

Richard walks back to the bar, where Kevin is waiting with some other Honda executives and a line of shots.

"This is the last shot I'm doing, man," Richard says. "I'm sticking with my Captain and Diet Coke."

Kevin continues to take more and more shots over the next thirty minutes while Richard nurses his one Captain and Diet Coke and talks with the Honda executives about his marketing rollout plan. Suddenly, a bump almost knocks Richard off his barstool. He turns and sees a large woman standing beside him with a drink in one hand and a guy standing right behind her, who has a horribly ugly tattoo design of a dragon on his arm. She mutters to Richard, "Hey, my friend over there likes you."

"Which friend?" Richard replies, hoping she's not talking about the guy who is with her.

"Her, the thin blond," the large woman says. Richard turns to look around the lady and sees a woman staring at him with a big smile.

The blond woman is about ten years older than Richard and has a thin figure without any curves. She is wearing a short miniskirt and tight shirt that exposes her bare shoulders. She has huge bright blue eyes.

"Okay," Richard says with a little chuckle in his voice. "Thank you, but I'm married." Richard flashes his wedding ring that he is wearing on his left hand. The large lady persists and asks Richard to dance.

"Listen, honey," Richard says, showing off his sexy grin. "I'm just here with my friend having a few drinks and then we're off." With that, the large woman turns her nose up and walks off with the tattooed guy.

"Shit, I think that blond is hot, dude," Kevin blurts out.

"You would," mutters Richard.

"Yeah, I'm buying her a shot," Kevin says.

"Hey, sweetheart," Kevin yells as he starts calling for the bartender to come down to his end of the bar. As he tries to get the bartender's attention, two young blond girls, both with large breasts almost falling out of their tops, walk up to the bar holding trays of shots. Now that the bar is crowded, the bartender is too busy at the other end helping others and doesn't even glance over in Kevin's direction. The bartender looks to be in her late twenties, and she is extremely attractive with dark brown hair and big fake breasts. It's no wonder why Kevin, who has been married and divorced three times, wants her to send some more attention his way.

The girls holding the trays of shots ask in unison, "Would you like a shot of vodka and Red Bull?"

Kevin and the Honda execs take one look at these girls and in unison say, "Sure, we'd love one." The Honda execs and Kevin turn and look at each other while Kevin buys the shots.

"Hey, big man," Kevin says while staring at Richard. "Ready for another, bro?"

"No, man, I'm moving to water now," Richard says.

The bartender finally makes it over to Kevin after about 20 minutes go by. "Hey, honey," Kevin says to the bartender, who gives him a dirty look. "I need water for the little baby next to me here, and, while you're at it, can you please take his man card? Yeah!" Kevin and all the Honda execs start laughing.

The bartender pours the water from her sprayer and places it in front of Richard. She then leans over and says, "Hey, do you know that someone in here likes you?"

"Yes. Let me guess. Is it that blond older lady over there with the blue eyes?" Richard replies almost sarcastically as he looks toward the lady in question, who is now on the dance floor with her very large lady friend, her guy friend with the tattoo, another dark-haired lady, and some random older guy.

"Yep," the bartender replies, and then walks away.

Richard looks over at the group dancing. The large woman who came over before with the ugly tattoo guy thinks Richard is checking them out, so she takes his glances as an invitation to come walking over again.

"Let's go! Time to dance!" she says as she walks up and grabs Richard's arm, trying to pull him onto the dance floor.

Richard, who doesn't want to make a scene in front of the Honda executives, can clearly tell that the lady is now a lot drunker than she was forty minutes ago when she first approached him. He allows her to pull him to the dance floor, where the blond blue-eyed older lady is simultaneously dancing, taking the shot Kevin just brought her, and waiting for Richard with a huge smile on her face.

"Hello," she says as Richard nears. "I've been watching you all night."

"Oh really? That is very flattering," Richard says, "but I told your friend that I'm married and have two children."

"I know. She told me," the woman says seductively, "but I don't mind. I'm not looking for a husband. I already have one of those."

Richard tries to dance for about thirty seconds with her but just says, "Sorry, I just can't dance right now. I'm not drunk enough, sorry." He walks off and heads back to the bar where he left Kevin and the Honda execs.

However, when Richard gets back to the bar, he realizes that Kevin and the Honda execs are gone. Richard walks to the bathroom, thinking maybe the guys are in there. After all, he's only been gone for a minute. The bathroom is so small with just one stall, a single sink, and one urinal. He goes into the bathroom stall, uses the facility, comes out, and washes his hands, yet he doesn't see any of Honda execs or Kevin in the tiny bathroom. Richard then walks back out to the main area. He looks around for a while standing in place and spinning around, casing the entire bar. He sees no one.

"Great," Richard mutters to himself. He pulls out his cell phone and calls Kevin. Ring, ring, ring, ring—no answer. He just gets Kevin's voice mail. Richard walks back to his barstool at the wood bar and starts texting Kevin: "Hey dude where are you?" The bartender walks back over, and Richard asks her if she's seen his friends.

"No, but here is their tab," she says. She lays out a bill for about $840 that Richard now has to pay.

"Great, Kevin the responsible," Richard mutters again. It's no big deal, however. It's all getting charged to the company account. It's just that they don't like it when employees spend money on alcohol, even if it helps land a deal.

"Okay, here's my credit card," Richard says. "But, wait. Go ahead and throw one more Captain and Diet Coke on their before you close it up. Thanks."

Richard pays the bill and gets his drink. For the next thirty minutes Richard keeps checking his phone to see if there are any voicemails, texts, and emails from Kevin while the ice is melting in his drink. He is just about to start drinking it when the blond, blue-eyed older lady comes up to him and says, "Well, looks like you are all alone. Do you need a ride?"

"No thanks," Richard says. "I'm staying at a hotel not far from here."

"Ooh, you already have a hotel room ready for us," the blond says with a sexy little smile.

"No, no, no. I just need to find my friends and leave," Richard states.

"Well, are you sure you're not up for a long night of hot sex tonight with a woman you don't know?" The blond questions him as she presses her small breasts and flat body up against Richard's.

"No thanks, honey," Richard says with a nervous laugh. "You have a good night, because I have a meeting in the morning and I really must go."

He slugs his Captain Morgan and Diet Coke and slams his empty glass on the bar. Then Richard grabs his receipt, folds it, and puts it into his wallet.

"Wait!" says the bartender. "Listen, I know you're not from around here, but in this county, we have no crime and no problems."

"So what…good for you guys," Richard says.

"Well, the police around here have nothing to do but pull people over, and they are looking to give DUIs and I thought you should know," the bartender says as she slides another water across the bar to Richard.

He looks up into the red neon Red Bull sign just above the bar behind her and has a flashback, thinking back on an incident in which he fell in a parking lot drunk while walking to his car. Richard then remembers trying to put his car key into the car door, but missing while drunk and then falling forward onto the car door. He then remembers still trying to get his key working, but this time in the car ignition. His next memory is driving drunk with only one eye open and then nodding off behind the wheel, almost slamming into a guardrail. Richard's final memory is of him standing in front of a Miami officer clearly drunk and laughing with his feet spread apart and arms out trying to touch his nose. The Miami officer said, "Richard, I'm going to let you go with just a minor ticket, but you need to let him drive." The officer pointed to Kevin, who was laughing and sitting in the passenger seat of Richard's car wearing the blinking Coca-Cola button and a Dolphins Football hat.

His mind back in the present, Richard looks at the Red Bull sign once again and then stands in front of the bartender. "Don't worry, I've drunk way more than this with no problems and been on water for awhile," he says. He then walks out of the bar to his rental car.

CHAPTER FOUR

ONCE IN the vehicle, Richard tries again to call Kevin several times, but never gets an answer. As Richard begins to drive around, he realizes that he may be a little lost. He didn't pay too much attention to his surroundings when he was on the way to the bar because he followed Kevin in his car and never thought he would be leaving without him. As Richard drives, he goes under a tunnel, says to himself, "This looks familiar," and begins to search for road signs that look like the ones that he used when following Kevin to get to the bar.

As Richard continues to drive around, slowly looking for his way out of downtown, he makes a turn into a parking lot by accident and sees a police car sitting there with just the inside map lights on, the police office inside reading. Richard immediately starts sweating and pulls out of the parking lot, still trying to find his way to a familiar road and thinking about what the bartender said to him on his way out of the bar.

After about fifteen minutes go by with no other vehicles in sight, Richard finally finds Abraham Street, which looks very familiar. He makes a left turn and starts driving through what looks like a residential neighborhood, but it appears at the end to be heading onto the highway. Halfway down Abraham Street, an SUV passes Richard going the opposite way. Richard's phone rings; it's Kevin.

"Hey bro, I just passed you. Where you going?" Kevin asks him.

"Well, since you abandoned me at the bar, I decided to leave, but I got a little lost coming out of that damn place," Richard tells him.

"No, no, no!" Kevin says. "Turn around and come back to bar with me, man."

"No, I really can't, bro," Richard replies. "I got a flight tomorrow morning at 10:30, and you know that's an all-day plane ride back to Florida."

"Listen, pussy, you never come out here, and we haven't hung out in a while," Kevin blurts out. "Get your ass back here!"

"Okay, okay, fine I'll turn around," Richard says.

"So where the hell were you?" Richard asks him.

"Bro, I walked outside to call my wife, and this young hot drunk girl asks me for a ride," Kevin explains as he starts to laugh. "So I immediately say to her, 'No problem, hop in my car.'"

"Wait, wait, wait a minute," Richard yells. "Some drunken girl just walks up to you outside the bar and asks you for a ride home? And that's it?" Richard asks.

"Well, two guys came around looking for her, and she appeared to be trying to get away from them, so I told her I would take her home," Kevin explains further.

"Okay, bullshit, but continue," Richard says, laughing.

"Anyway, while in the car, she couldn't remember where she lived, so we drove around for a few minutes, and then I took her to my place in the city," boasts Kevin.

"Hold on!" Richard yells. "You drove around for a minute and then you took her to your place? Dude, are you fucking crazy? Why would you take a drunk girl that doesn't know where she lives back to your place?" Richard asks him with an increasingly raised voice.

"Well, she didn't remember where she lived, so I had to take her somewhere," Kevin explains very seriously. "Besides, when she got to my place, she started to freak out a little bit."

"Yeah, ya think? She probably thought you were going to fucking rape her, you asshole." Richard says. "She's in some strange much older dude's apartment that she doesn't know. I'm sure she thought you were supposed to take her home." Richard continues to yell.

"Hey screw you dude, I'm only a few years older than you. Anyway, look, then after we left, she figured out where she lived, and I took her right there." Blurts Kevin.

"Buddy, why didn't you just call her a cab when you met her outside in the first place, you idiot?" Richard yells.

"I thought I was helping her." Kevin is almost in tears from laughing.

"Shit, I got to go. Cops are all over here. See you back at the bar in a second," Richard says.

"Okay, it's just ahead. Make a left and then it will be right on your left," Kevin explains to him.

Richard hangs up the phone and puts his signal on to make a left turn. The light just ahead is red. He pulls all the way up to the line on the street just before the crosswalk. A cop car is just sitting there across the way on the left, facing Richard in the direction he is going to turn. The light remains red while all the lights around the other parts of the intersection turn green and then red again. The light rotation goes through three more times, never turning green for him.

"Shit," Richard says aloud. "What the fuck is wrong with this damn light? Why won't it turn?

"Crap, I can't turn left on red, I can't cross lanes at an intersection, and I can't back up without getting pulled over to make sure I'm on the crossbar," he says to himself. "I'm screwed."

Then suddenly the cop's traffic light turns green again, and the cop goes and turns right toward him. Richard gazes in his rearview mirror only to see the cop make a U-turn and get immediately behind his stopped rental car. Then the light finally turns green for Richard. He starts driving, and as he makes his left turn, police lights immediately begin to flash.

"Fuck, like I need this shit," Richard yells out inside the car.

As Richard begins to pull his car to the side, he thinks to himself, "What if I pull over to the side and run? There is a fence right there, and a train yard beyond it." He imagines jumping out of the vehicle and starting to run toward the fence that is in front of the train yard. He then imagines hopping the fence while the officer, who is too slow to catch him and make it over the fence himself, falls behind. Richard then takes off his sweaty shirt and walks back to the bar where he greets Kevin, who is already sitting there with two shots waiting for them. Back at his rental car, a police officer searches the trunk and finds Richard's briefcase that has his name monogrammed on the inside. The next day, a band of local officers surround Smothers Advertising Agency and pull Richard out of a meeting with Mr. Smothers and place in him handcuffs. Sacramento police must have tipped them off.

Back to reality, Richard stops the car on the right side of the street near a walkway. The cop has his bright spotlight turned on and faces the light toward Richard's vehicle. The officer then walks up to Richard's car door holding a flashlight and waving it around like a cocky bastard.

"Hey, where are you going, son?" Officer Allen asks.

"Well, Officer, I'm going to this bar called Mix to pick up my friend who can't drive because he drank too much," Richard explains.

"Really? Well, we get a lot of people doing that here for friends," Officer Allen states. "Have you been drinking tonight at all?" Officer Allen asks in a friendly manner.

"Yes, I had a glass of wine at dinner and two after-dinner drinks."

"Oh really? And at what time did you have dinner?"

"Well…" Richard checks his watch. It's about midnight. "I think it was about four hours ago, around eight o'clock," Rich explains soft voice.

"Where did you go to dinner, and at what time did you stop drinking your after-dinner drinks?" questions Officer Allen.

"Well, we went to Karver's Steakhouse in Roseville, and now I'm going to pick up my friend who cannot drive. My last drink was at eleven and then I drank some water," Richard tells him. "I got a little lost over here. I'm from Florida, and these kind of narrow one-way city streets are a little confusing here."

"Yeah, great, especially after twelve o'clock in the morning," barks Officer Allen. "I need to see your license, and I need you to step out of the vehicle."

CHAPTER FIVE

THE RAIN and roar of thunder appear to be getting louder back at Officer Allen's house.

"Do you remember that night, Officer Allen? Do you remember what you put me through, the treatment you gave me? Do you realize what it cost me for being over a street cross bar? No, no, no, you don't," Richard speaks softly with a crazed sound in his voice.

With Richard now standing in front of his car on the side of the alleyway street, Officer Allen asks him to spread his legs apart and put his arms out straight. Richard is a little chilly, since it's about fifty-two degrees, and he is used to the warm Miami weather. Next, Officer Allen asks Richard to walk in a straight line heel-toe-heel-toe, which he completes flawlessly.

"Now, recite the alphabet backward for me, Richard," barks Officer Allen. He is a little slow, but Richard manages to do a good job saying the alphabet backward.

"Now, I want you to hold one leg up at a time as high as you can and for as long as you can, okay?" Officer Allen speaks in a soft voice and barely looks at Richard. Instead, he is admiring Richard's new Hyundai Genesis rental vehicle.

Richard, who is now shivering a little, says, "Officer Allen, on top of it being a little cold out tonight, I really have bad balance."

"Well, just do it for as long as you can," barks Officer Allen again.

Richard lifts his left leg first as high as he can and then drops it down.

"No, no, no! I want you to lift your leg and count while you are doing it," Officer Allen spits the order.

Richard begins to lift his leg again, and this time he counts to about twenty-four before he puts his leg down.

"Okay, next leg."

Richard lifts his right leg and begins to count. He only gets to about fourteen before dropping the leg.

"Pick it up, do it again, and count from where you left off."

Richard lifts his leg once again, begins counting at fifteen, and this time gets to about thirty-four.

"Okay, now come here," says Officer Allen, who is walking toward the rear passenger door of his police car. "Blow into this." He holds up a breathalyzer device.

Richard remembers a story that one of his buddies told him in the past about always refusing to perform a breathalyzer test. So, he replies, "No, I prefer not to take it."

Immediately Officer Allen throws the breathalyzer device into the backseat of the police car and turns Richard around, pushing him up against the police car, cuffing him, and then placing him in the back of the vehicle. Officer Allen then jumps into Richard's rental vehicle. Richard looks through the metal shroud from the backseat of Officer Allen's police car, wondering what's going on. Officer Allen then drives the rental vehicle and parks it in a nearby parking spot close to the sidewalk, where Richard originally pulled off the road. Officer Allen then jumps back into his car and says, "Video off."

Richard, who doesn't even know what's happening, says, "Officer, these cuffs are pinching my skin. Why are you doing this? Isn't there another way to work this out?"

"You refused to take the breathalyzer test, so now we'll go down to jail, and either you'll take it there or I'll take your blood."

"Officer," Richard says with worry in his voice. "I'm in town from Florida working on a huge campaign for American Honda. If word of this gets out, I'll be fired. Can't you help me?"

"No, a big executive like you I'm sure they won't fire," Office Allen says with a smirk on his face that Richard can see through the rearview mirror. "Listen, if you pass the test, then I'll drive you back to your car."

After thirty minutes in the cold and a ten-minute car ride later, they arrive at the jail. Officer Allen pulls Richard out of the vehicle and places him in a concrete area with a concrete bench and a half-wall that hosts another concrete bench on the other side.

"Sit down here," barks Officer Allen with a smirk on his face. Allen walks away and starts to ask Richard questions in a loud, condescending manner. "Age, weight, height, primary language, and waist size." Then he begins to ask Richard if he has a drinking or drug problem, or whether he will go into shock from drug or alcohol withdrawal. Richard answers no to all of the questions and looks at Officer Allen like he's crazy for even asking such questions in the first place.

Just as Officer Allen seems to be finished interrogating Richard, another officer walks in with an older man who is staggering and handcuffed. The man is large and burly, and he is huffing and puffing like he's trying to the blow the concrete wall down. Richard peers over at the man in complete fear.

"Officer, what is that guy doing?" Richard mutters.

"Ignore him," Officer Allen says. "He thinks if he continues to do that he'll pass the breathalyzer test."

"Really? Does it work?" Richard questions.

"Nooooooo," yells Officer Allen.

Allen now walks over with a needle in one hand and rubber gloves in the other.

"Boy, which one will it be—the breathalyzer or the needle?" Officer Allen chuckles and smirks at Richard.

"I hate needles, so I guess the breathalyzer," Richard replies in an almost boyish voice.

Officer Allen uncuffs Richard. There is a red ring around both of his wrists and a little scrape of blood. Richard grabs his wrists and rubs them as he walks over to the breathalyzer device that Officer Allen has in his hand.

"Is there any way to work this out?" Richard asks politely.

"Well, you could try bribing us," Officer Allen says while he and the other officer chuckle.

"Well, something tells me that might not be the right thing to do."

"Well, if not, then put your mouth on the end of this and blow."

Richard places his mouth on the end of the breathalyzer device and begins to blow.

"Blow, blow, blow!" yells Officer Allen.

Richard watches as the light on the breathalyzer device turns from green to yellow.

"Keep going! Push! Almost there. Keep blowing, harder, harder, harder! Yes!" says Officer Allen, laughing.

"Okay, one more time. Go!" screams Allen. "Go, blow hard!

"Harder, Harder, *Harder,*" screams Officer Allen.

"Well Richard, both results came out exactly the same—point zero eight one, which is point zero one one over the legal limit. Book him," Officer Allen tells another officer as he walks away and hands Richard over.

"But wait! Why, why?" Richard asks. "I didn't even drink that much. Why didn't you give me a break before you tested me again?

"This seems like a setup!" Richard screams.

The booking officer says in a very soft-spoken manner with his head hanging down, "Can you please follow me, sir?" The officer removes all of the items from Richard's pockets before taking Richard's mug shot and fingerprints.

Still with a soft-spoken voice and his head hanging down, the officer says, "Sir, you will have to stay in this holding cell for about an hour and a half. However, there is a phone in here for you to make any local calls. Then, I will put you in a permanent cell for another three hours, and finally after that you will be released.

"Please remove your shoes and place them just outside your door here," the booking officer tells Richard.

Without any sound and just a fiery look on his face, Richard takes off his shoes and places them just outside the door as he's told. He then walks into the holding cell and plops down on the hard mattress that is sitting on a concrete platform. The holding cell is a concrete block with gray jailhouse paint. There is a metal toilet at the opposite end of the bed, and beside it a phone.

The only opening is a horizontal slit in the middle of the door that his eyes can just peer through.

Since he doesn't have his cell phone, Richard cannot look up any phone numbers to let Kevin or anybody else know that he has been arrested. As he sits and stares at the concrete gray wall, all can he think about is why him. He replays the situation back in his mind, wondering why he turned around in the first place to go back, questioning where the hell Kevin really went and why he really wanted Richard to turn around. Could he have done anything else differently to not be here right now? What if he hadn't had that last Captain Morgan and Diet at the end? What if he had accepted the ride home with the thin blue-eyed blond woman? What if he had never gone out at all? What if he had bought that breathalyzer test that he seen in the *Sky Magazine* on the plane and had it shipped to his hotel room? What's going to happen when Honda and Mr. Smothers find out about his arrest?

An hour and a half goes by, and the soft-spoken booking officer opens the door and says, "Sir, follow me. It will be all right."

Richard looks around, and there are six other doors with shoes outside of them.

"I'm going to lose my job," Richard says with a bit of cottonmouth, finally breaking his silence.

"Well, I hope not, sir. You'll be all right," the officer tells him. "I need to put you in here for three hours, and then I'll let you go."

The new cell is much bigger than the holding cell. However, Richard knows by looking around inside that this new cell is usually used for holding all sorts of criminals. The cell has light brown faded paint on the walls with some graffiti. There is also a little smudge or two of blood. The cell also has a metal toilet in it. One different item it has is a red button on the wall near the cell entrance called a call box. Richard knows that the call box is new because it is clean and looks out of place. The new cell also has bunk beds, but thankfully, for Richard's sake, he is all alone in there. The bed's plastic thin mattress feels to him like he is lying on crushed bugs. As Richard attempts to lie down and get some rest, the mattress begins to make him itch. Richard feels beaten and gross. Even through the rough mental anguish and treatment he's been subjected to, he still manages to curl into a ball and lie down on the plastic crunchy bug mattress that sits on the bottom concrete bunk. Time seems to stand still in this cell, and after an hour and a half Richard starts to feel a little claustrophobic and runs over to the call button and presses it. On the other end of the speaker, he hears the booking officer immediately say, "You still have an hour and a half left, sir."

"Shit, really?" Richard almost cries as he sits down on the plastic bunk mattress, his head in his hands.

Richard left his phone in the rental car, and during his arrest Kevin sent him a series of text messages:

"dude are you ok?"

"dude did you get stopped?"

"dude did you get picked up?"

"dude do you need me to bail you out?"

"dude should I call Mr. Smothers and let him know?"

"dude call me."

Richard continues to play the night back in his head over and over again. *Should I have run? No, because my briefcase was in the trunk. Should I have grabbed my briefcase and then run and jumped the fence? No, it would have taken too long, and the briefcase is too heavy and would have weighed me down, and Officer Allen would have caught me on the fence while trying to jump it. What if I had kept driving to the hotel and never looked back? Yeah, I could be sleeping on a real bed in a hotel right now instead of this fleabag cell.*

Then, in his mind, Richard starts wondering *Why? Why didn't that light change? Why did Officer Allen wait until three light rotations to stop me? Why did Kevin take that girl home? Why weren't the Honda executives still at the bar? Why didn't I stay at the bar longer? Why did I even go out after dinner? Why did Officer Allen give me all of those tests knowing he was going to arrest me anyway? Why did he pinch my wrists with the handcuffs? Why do I feel like I was set up?*

"Okay, you can leave," says a loud voice over the metal speaker box in the jail cell. The metal door opens up automatically, and Richard walks out and puts on his sneakers that are sitting outside the cell. He looks to the left, which is a narrow hallway with a door at the end. He then looks to the right, where an officer is standing behind a glass door pointing at Richard to move forward to his left. As he begins to walk, he feels dizzy, tired, and mentally drained. When he comes to the door, he opens it.

A little glass window with a hole and ledge is in front of him. Another officer stands behind the glass and says to him, "Okay, here is what you brought in. One wallet, one wedding ring, one car key, one room key, and one watch."

Richard looks up only to see a faint reflection of himself in the glass and replies, "Thanks." The reflection shows Richard with his left eye all red, appearing to have a little blood in it.

"Go out that door in front of you," snarls the officer. Richard hits the bar on the door as hard as he can to open it, causing the door to make a loud boom like thunder crashing.

CHAPTER SIX

RICHARD SITS Indian style next to Officer Allen's wife back in their house during the thunderstorm.

"So, Mrs. Allen, does something sound strange here?" Richard removes the tape from her mouth.

"Take a look at that sweet innocent man you call husband and father over there." Mrs. Allen looks over to her husband as she tries to stifle her tears.

"*Right!*" Richard yells. Lighting crashes outside the cathedral windows.

As Richard walks outside the jail, he looks around, but nobody is in sight. It's about four fifty in the morning, and there are hardly any lights on outside, and the air is a little damp. There are no other officers, no taxicabs waiting for fares like he remembers seeing in movies, and no people. So Richard walks around the jail looking for someone, but he begins to get in a little bit of a panic. He tries to open the door he just came out of, but he discovers that it's locked. He walks to the parking lot only to find empty police cars parked there, but no one in sight. He stumbles back up the wet, grassy hill and sees a set of stairs to his left. Richard walks up the stairs to what appears to be another building attached to the jail. He tries the door and it opens.

Richard cautiously walks in, looking around and saying, "Hello, anybody here?" No answer. He continues to walk through the hallway, which is narrow but not too narrow. On his left are ceiling-to-floor glass windows facing the outside, and on his right are individual glass offices with files stacked up against the glass, only small portions of the offices showing above the stacks.

Finally, he comes across another window that looks similar the one that the officer who checked him out of the jail stood behind, though this one has a much smaller window and instead has a phone on the outside lying on a small shelf. The phone is older, beige in color, and has six buttons along the bottom with one button pushed in indicated by a red light. Richard picks up the phone and says "Hello" with an almost boyish-sounding voice. He hears no answer on the other end, so Richard presses another button and says "Hello" again, but still receives no answer. He then proceeds to press the other three buttons, and after pressing the last button, someone finally answers on the other end. "*Hello*," Richard yells.

Immediately he hears Christmas music playing: "Jingle Bell Rock." Richard thinks how odd this is considering that it's February. He slams the phone down, and in a sweaty panic he goes running back out the front door and down the stairs through the police parking lot and out the front gate of the jail. He walks through the wet grass to a nearby sidewalk illuminated by low-lit streetlights. He looks to his left, which looks dark, and then to the right, where he sees a little bit of light in the distance. Richard immediately begins to run as fast as he can toward the light. He's physically and mentally drained from being awake for over twenty-four hours, but he manages to conjure up enough stamina to make it to the light. He is a little frightened, since the area isn't the nicest and he doesn't know if he is going the right way to find his vehicle. Finally, though, as he gets closer to the light, he sees a big gas station.

Once at the gas station, Richard walks in, sweaty with his dress pants soaked at the bottom from the wet grass and his dirty sweaty dress shirt un-tucked. He walks down one of the aisles toward the back of the gas station. He grabs a cold bottle of water from behind a glass case. Water in hand, Richard walks up to the gas station clerk, who looks like he might have spent a couple of nights in Richard's cell himself. The gas station attendant is a big, burly man with several tattoos on his arms and long blondish-brown hair. His overgrown beard appears as though the man hasn't bathed in two weeks. Still out of breath, Richard pays for his water, despite the fact that his looks seem to say that he can't afford it. Then, Richard asks the attendant if he can call a cab for him. Richard exhausted and tired had no idea where he was or how to get back to his rental car. The attendant agrees, but just then Richard hears a crash and spins around to find the source of the sound and check out if anyone else is in the gas station.

"Well, Mrs. Allen," Richard says in a soft voice. He begins to raise his volume slowly. "Thankfully, my car was *Only Two Fucking Miles Away!*"

Richard gets up and hits Officer Allen across the face with the side of his gun. Allen falls a little forward to the right, but rotates back up with some blood now dripping from his head. Richard then goes back to using a soft voice and asks the children if they would like the glass of water that he recently poured. As the children sip on the water, Richard continues to explain to Mrs. Allen that he couldn't sleep when he got back to his hotel because he couldn't stop wondering what he was going to tell Mr. Smothers.

"I was saying aloud, 'how can I swing this?' That's all I kept saying. 'How can I swing this to not lose my job?' So here is the best part," Richard says as he raises the gun again and places it back on Officer Allen's temple. "When I get home, my wife says to me—"

Back home in Miami, Rich and Mary are in the kitchen of their home sitting at the dinette table; it's pitch black outside.

"Great, I fucking told you not to give them any reason to fire you, but NOOO you had to fuck this up," Mary yells at Richard. "You better fucking pray that you can talk or sell your way out of this one Rich, 'cause I will not be humiliated in this goddamned community!"

"Aren't you even going to ask if I'm okay?" Rich says softly.

"No!" yells Mary as she slams her hand down on the glass dinette table.

CHAPTER SEVEN

LIGHTING CRASHES back at Officer Allen's house! With the gun still pointed at Officer Allen, Richard asks in almost at a whisper, "Do you believe that bitch after all that I gave her?" Richard gets off the elevator on his floor at Smothers Advertising Agency. As he walks off the elevator, the busy office almost stops and becomes silent. All eyes are on Richard as he slowly steps forward and proceeds to walk down between the row of cubicles on the left and the glass offices with no doors on the right. Toward the end of the long hallway is his large corner office. It is almost like Richard is in a fog; he can see everything, but he can only hear the whispers from his co-workers.

"Oh my God, it's him."

"Look, it's Rich."

"Fuck, that guy is screwed."

"He'll never get another gig in advertising."

"Ha ha, cocky bastard. I wonder if I can get his office."

"Sucks to be him."

"He was the only sexy thing to look at in this damn office."

"Nice knowing ya."

"Shit, I hope there won't be any more job cuts after this."

The hallway feels like it is never-ending. As Richard passes the cubicles, the peering eyes that fell upon him drop as the cubicle employees plop down in their chairs and pretend to type on their computers. As he passes the executive glass offices on the right side of the hallway, the standing executives hurry and pick up their office phones as if they are busy talking to someone on the other end. However, Richard doesn't hear the cubicle chairs creak as people plop down, he doesn't hear the typing sounds on computer keyboards, and he doesn't hear the other executives aggressively picking up the phones carrying on overly loud pretend phone conversations in their glass offices. Instead, Richard just hears the whispers.

Finally, as Richard reaches the end of the never-ending hallway, he peers around the corner only to notice that his secretary is not there even though it's not even five o'clock yet. He opens his big wooden door and enters his office, walking to his desk, which has a stunning view overlooking Bayside Marketplace in downtown Miami. He plops in his chair, swings it around to his computer, and attempts to log in. After repeated attempts with his password, Richard gives up, knowing now that all that is left is a phone call summoning him to Mr. Smothers' office. He swings his chair back around to the Bay and just sits there watching cruise boats enter and depart Bay Harbor, picking up passengers and dropping them off. Hours upon hours he sits just watching the cruise ships and waits for Mr. Smothers to finally call him up to his office.

Just as the sky turns orange and the sun begins to set, Richard halfway slides off his chair nodding off when he hears the sound of his office phone ringing.

"Hello," he answers, sounding as if he has a frog in his throat.

The deep voice that belongs to Mr. Smothers says over the phone, "Rich, I need you in my office."

Richard hangs up the phone, reluctantly placing the receiver back on its base.

Lighting crashes with a booming sound as if it just about struck the house as Richard sits next to Officer Allen crying.

"Well, let me tell you what happened next," cries Richard.

Richard presses the button in the elevator to go up to the penthouse floor. In almost fast-forward motion, he is now sitting down in Mr. Smothers's office with both Mr. Smothers and his brother sitting across from him behind a huge mahogany desk, ceiling-to-floor windows overlooking the whole city of Miami behind them. Both of the Smothers brothers are moving their lips, but Richard is in a daze and can't hear anything they are saying. To the left of Richard is Mr. Smothers's long-time assistant Betty, sitting on a beautiful white couch taking notes. Betty now about fifty-five had been Mr. Smothers's assistant since she was just twenty-six. Mr. Smothers always had a knack for attractive women ten years younger. Behind her to the right are two half-empty scotch glasses on the mahogany bar. Hours go by as the Smothers brothers explain why they have to let Richard go.

"Well Richard American Honda found out about your DUI and told us to drop you or they will drop us. They don't want their reputation tarnished by hiring an ad firm with the guy spear heading the project to have a DUI on his record," Alan Smothers says in stern voice. They stay up all night and into the morning discussing the matter at hand and getting up-to-date on all Richard's current projects including the American Honda deal.

After returning to his office and gathering up his things he realizes its *six o'clock* in the morning and the other employees are just starting to get into the office. Richard walks down the long hallway from his office with his last brown box of belongings as all the other office workers stare at him; they whisper to each other as he goes by, but Richard doesn't hear a thing. On a couple of computers in the cubicle area is Richard's mug shot from California; the state posts arrests online daily. Behind Richard, his old glass executive corner office now sits empty.

When Richard reaches the lobby of Smothers and Smothers Advertising, he presses the down button to the elevator. The door opens and the elevator is packed with Smothers and Smothers employees. Many of them notice that its Richard standing there with his box, yet each and every one of them look away from him in the opposite direction. All the way in the back, someone yells out, "Fuck this, I need to get this coffee to the conference room, so excuse me people." A swarm of people exits the elevator, nobody saying a word to Richard. The last person to exit the elevator is the coffee-carrying guy, who has both of his hands full of trays of coffee stacked on top of each other. He looks up from his coffee tower and says to Richard, "Tough break, man," and then walks out. Richard takes the elevator downstairs and then takes one last long look as he exits the building.

When he reaches his Honda Accord, he throws his brown box in and quickly drives off. Richard traded out of his Porsche for a Honda about six months ago when he was gathering research for the American Honda proposal. Richard figured that would be the best way to really understand the consumer if he owned American Honda's top selling vehicle. When he arrives back at home, it's still early morning. Richard walks up his driveway with one of his brown boxes. It's quiet in the neighborhood. All the kids are in school, husbands and wives are at work, and there is nothing but silence. The sun has just come up behind his house, and he can still see the morning dew glistening on the blades of grass. Richard opens the door to his house and immediately hears a woman saying, "*Yes, Oh Yes, Yes!*" As he walks closer and closer toward the sound, he sees a white sports bra lying on the floor. As he continues to walk down his hallway, he sees black spandex shorts lying across his kids' toy hobby-horse. The *"Yes, Yes, Oh Yes"* is getting extremely loud as Richard turns the corner into his kitchen. He then sees a perfectly fit young man in a tight blue spandex shirt that shows every toned muscle on his body and his bare un-tan white ass thrusting away. Legs straddle each side of him.

Richard says in an almost defeated voice, "Great."

"Oh shit," Mary says as she pops her head to the side around the trainer's huge bicep. The trainer immediately picks up his pants and runs out the back door, almost tripping because he can't get his pants up fast enough as they are sticking to his sweaty thighs.

Richard drops the brown box, walks upstairs, pulls a light blue suitcase from his closet, and starts to pack a couple of clothes and personal items. Mary, now covered with a robe, runs up the stairs, reaching Richard midway as he walks down the stairs carrying his suitcase.

"Rich, honey, I'm sorry," Mary cries.

"Save it, bitch," Richard barks back at her as he tries to squeeze by her on the stairs.

Mary trips over Richard's suitcase and falls down the stairs, sliding down the steps on her butt. At the bottom she sits and cries to Richard, "I'm sorry, don't leave. I'm sorry."

Richard steps over her at the bottom of the stairs and heads toward the front door with his suitcase. As he exits the front door, he looks back and Mary continues to sit in her robe at the bottom of the stairs crying. Then *Slam*! Richard shuts the door behind him.

CHAPTER EIGHT

"WELL, YOU see, Officer Allen, my whole life fell apart thanks to you." Richard pulls the trigger back on the gun he has aimed at Officer Allen's head.

"Mum, Mum, Mum, Mum," Officer Allen says, wiggling as a crackle of lighting can be heard outside the window.

"*What*!? Are you trying to say something, you piece of *Shit*?" Richard yells back at him. "You know what, *Officer*? I'm going to give you something I didn't have. You know what I'm going to give you? It's a chance to say bye to your family before it's all gone." His voice is soft but sadistic.

"That's right. My wife used that bullshit falling down the stairs issue, saying that I pushed her. She took the kids, the house, and all the money. Then she wasted no time in moving her personal trainer right in to my house. Yes, she really loved me. She even used the DUI against me, stating to the courts that I was a drunk and not fit to be a father and that I neglected her. I'm not even able to visit my own children, little Richy and Jenny. I know they are scared and miss me. I miss them and I haven't been able to see them in a month. She took everything, and at the end it was clear she just wanted the money not me. And now I can't even land a job," Richard says as he starts to cry.

Mrs. Allen bends over crying and snuggling up against her children and saying "No" in a whimpering voice.

Richard peels the tape off of Officer Allen's mouth, and with a big gasp, Officer Allen says, "Richard, you're right, you're right."

Mrs. Allen looks up at him, holding back tears as she stares blankly at her husband's face.

"You're right, you were set up. I'm sorry, but you're right," Officer Allen says, crying.

"Bullshit, you little fuck. Oh, *now* I'm fucking right after all this," Richard screams. "Come on, Officer Allen. You've got to give me more than that, bitch. I'll make you eat this fucking gun." Enraged Richard proceeds to put the gun in Officer Allen's mouth.

"*Wait*!" Officer Allen yells at him. "Listen, I'm not proud of this at all." His voice reveals his humility.

Mrs. Allen stands up. She has almost no tears now with the exception of those that have dried on her cheeks. With her hands bound, she charges her husband. Richard grabs her as she begins to kick Officer Allen in the stomach, lifting her up and pulling her away and back to the floor where she was sitting.

"Again. I can't believe it. Fucking again. The whole time," Mrs. Allen yells out to her husband. "He was right, he was right, and *you're* sorry? You put us through this crap, and the whole time he was right, you motherfucker! I warned you one day this shit would come back and haunt us."

"Look, there are a lot of things involved here," Officer Allen says.

"Yeah? I'm listening," Richard states.

"For one, I needed some more arrests, or I was going to be out of a job. Do you realize that we are cutting back the police force by forty percent in Sacramento? Forty percent! The police force of all things, for Christ's sake?" Allen's voice is casual but stern. "The state is out of money, and policemen, firemen, and teachers are being cut across the board. I had to do what I had to do to you for my family, and I'm sorry, but I needed to do it." Officer Allen speaks with a strict tone in his voice as he looks toward his wife.

Richard is now on the ground on his knees with the gun holding his body up as he presses the barrel to the ground with his hand. He looks as if he is doing a one-arm pushup. He is in total shock that Officer Allen is confessing the truth. Richard has so much anger and adrenaline rushing through his body that pushing the gun into the floor is the only way he can contain himself. Mrs. Allen starts yelling again at her husband.

"Look what you did to this poor man! Do you see what you did to his life? Is this worth it? Look at what you brought him to! He lost his job, his wife, his kids—everything. Look at what you put *us* through!"

Richard begins to untie Mrs. Allen and the children as she keeps barking at her husband.

"Seriously, are you fucking joking with me? Did the police force really make you that insensitive toward everything?" she questions her husband. "I mean, gosh, I sure as hell noticed it made you not care about this family—you know, us here." Mrs. Allen points to herself and their children.

Officer Allen has a baffled looks on his face. "I don't know what to say. I haven't been insensitive, have I?"

"We barely exist to you anymore," Mrs. Allen says definitively.

"Look, some of us set up these DUI stings around places where people could be drinking, ya know," Officer Allen explains as he tries to justify his actions. "You know, it keeps the cash pumping through the…"

"*Wait*!" Richard raises his voice. "You said that there were many things involved. Tell me what else," says Rich with that sexy grin. Officer Allen swallows hard as if he is downing a golf ball. He then begins to retell the events of the night.

"Well, I was staking out the club like I always do for potential drunk drivers and noticed you walking outside and looking around. After about thirty or forty minutes, you came back out again, jumped into this car, and drove off. I began to try and follow you, but I got caught behind this truck stopped at the railroad tracks, so I set up my wireless transmitter at the cross-road. Anyway, I guess you got lost because I noticed you heading back toward me after about fifteen minutes. I was stopped at the light with my wireless transmitter in place. I noticed Richard had pulled past the deceiving double crossbar a little, so I used the transmitter to prevent the light from turning green. Finally, after four light rotations, I broke the wireless connection, turned my light green, and turned right toward you, who then began to back up behind the first crossbar. I then immediately pulled behind you and stopped you for pulling past the crossbar and backing up."

There is a flash of lightning as the storm continues outside. Richard is on the floor in the house with his arm flexed holding onto the gun in a pushup position, his head facing down to the tile floor, his eyes wide open as if he is looking at something. His body is now extended flat with his chest hovering off the ground and his legs apart. Richard's body is so stiff, and his face and teeth are clinched together as if he is about to explode in rage. He is pushing all his negative energy towards the ground instead bursting and taking his rage out on Officer Allen.

Richard's mind flashes back to the scene with Officer Allen smirking as he gave Richard the road sobriety test. He then recalls Officer Allen cuffing him and throwing him into the backseat of his cop car. Richard then thinks back to Officer Allen laughing as he has Richard blow into the breathalyzer device at the local jail. Thinking back on their conversation, Richard remembers Officer Allen telling him, "You could try bribing us."

Lightning strikes and thunder booms throughout the house. Richard pushes the gun hard to the tile, propelling himself upward. He stands up and lunges aggressively toward Officer Allen, his face looking like it is chiseled out of rock, his teeth crunched together tightly.

Richard yells louder than he ever has, "*Wait a Fucking Minute.*" He then points the gun back toward Officer Allen, his finger on the trigger trembling from the rush of adrenaline that has overtaken him. "There are way too many holes in this bullshit story. Now you fucking tell me what really happened, or I'll barbecue your ass and let your wife light the goddamned match."

Sweat runs down Officer Allen's face. He is still on his knees but completely upright and stiff as a board. Richard has the gun on Officer Allen's temple, his finger trembling on the trigger ready to fire. Mrs. Allen is in complete shock, her hair frizzy and her makeup running. There is nothing left but dried tears, sweat, and runny makeup lines on her face. For the first time tonight, Mrs. Allen knows that the next words out of her husband's mouth could be his last, as she too notices Richard's finger trembling on the trigger.

"We rigged the breathalyzer test," a stuttering Officer Allen says as he releases a large poof as if he had been holding his breath in for a long time.

Exhausted from holding his breath, Officer Allen falls partially forward and then eases back down to sit on his knees.

"Yeah," Richard says as his finger releases the trigger of the gun and extends gently onto the barrel slide. The gun is still pressed against Officer Allen's temple.

"Well, it's quite easy, actually," Officer Allen explains. "We set the machine point zero two higher to start, so whatever you blew would automatically be point zero two higher than you were. Yeah," Officer Allen says with a mild laugh. "The only way to get caught is to have a court order for our equipment to be inspected, but all the judges and county employees are in on it. So, if we ever have to get it checked out, nobody would tell that it's faulty or that is has been tampered with because we would adjust it back before the inspection, since we would be tipped off ahead of time that someone is coming to check." Officer Allen tells the story with a sense of pride, and even giggles a little.

Richard grunts and pushes the barrel harder against Officer Allen's temple. Mrs. Allen, who is now standing behind Richard, gives her husband a snide look.

"Well…" says Officer Allen as Richard pushes the gun barrel against his head and moves it slightly to the left. Once again, Officer Allen sounds like he is holding his breath just a little when speaking.

"Great, a bunch of corrupt police, officials, and county employees," Richard says with a kind of defeated voice. "What else?"

"What do you mean, 'what else'?" Officer Allen asks, his voice crackling and a little high-pitched.

"I mean, what else? 'Cause this is a really fucking nice house you have here, Officer. Your wife doesn't work," Richard says in a calm voice as he removes the gun from Officer Allen's temple. He then looks around the house, waving the gun with his right hand toward the large living room space. He looks toward Mrs. Allen. "Come on! *What Else?*" Richard barks loudly.

"Well, I do some moonlighting work sometimes," Officer Allen confesses with the high-pitched crackle in his voice again.

"*Oh Yeah?* Like what?" Richard demands, pointing the gun at Allen's head.

"Well, you know some people have problems getting little things done, so I help push things just a bit so it can work out. That's all," Officer Allen says very softly.

"Who are your clients?" Richard asks him, a nasty undertone in his voice.

"Mostly business executives, you know." Officer Allen's eyes wander off.

"What kind of business executives, Officer?" Richard grinds his teeth.

"Corporate executives from out of town from different companies like manufacturers of products to advertising agencies."

"Okay. I want to know who hired you to nail me, and I want to know right fucking now!" Richard says while grinding his teeth. He slides his finger back onto the trigger.

"Oookay, listen. I'll tell you what you want to know, but please just let us all go. I won't even report this," Officer Allen stutters.

"Listen, either you tell me now, or the last thing you are going to hear is the chamber of my gun," Richard says definitively.

"Look, I helped this guy out once before on a small problem that he had with an airline executive. It was no big deal and nobody got hurt," Officer Allen explains. "Besides, he was a referral from some guys who own some of the local bars. In fact, one of the bars was the one you were at that night."

Richard thinks back to his car ride with Kevin when he just arrived in California. "But, hey, nice job on landing that executive jet airliner company," Richard remembers telling Kevin.

"*Kevin*," Richard says to Officer Allen, an overwhelming look of shock on his face.

Officer Allen smiles and says, "Yeah, good old Kevin. He sure is a funny son-of-a bitch, right?"

Richard puts the gun down to his side and says, "Tell me everything—slowly." Lightning flashes once again, making Richard's face look semi-sadistic.

CHAPTER NINE

LIGHTING CRASHES outside the house as Officer Allen explains.

"Well, one night I was hammered sitting at a local bar with a bunch of these bar owners that I was telling you about. You know, they were giving me free drinks. These guys know how to party. They always have the hottest barmaids and sexiest shot girls. I mean, these guys throw mad cash around to some of the younger new hires. These guys got these women giving them blowjobs in their private limos. I mean, one girl must have blown all five of these guys that night.

"Anyway, so we are all hanging out laughing, drinking, and bullshitting, as always. We all were drinking a ton, and they were talking about all the deals with businesses and local banks they have lined up to buy some more bars and clubs in town that were having some financial concerns, ya know."

Officer Allen says, "I remember being outside another club with its owner, who was being arrested for allowing minors in his club."

The club owner asked, "But how?"

Officer Allen remembers smirking and pushing the club owner's head down as he pushed him into the backseat of his police car. "Yeah, save it, my friend," he said. "We got an anonymous tip that you were letting minors in."

"Yeah, now some of these other owners were forced to sell due to their new troubles with local law enforcement. So one night we were all at this bar bullshitting, and then Big Joe, the main guy, yells across the bar, 'Well, was she a fucking Hoover or what?' He laughs as he hugs this guy I have seen before but never really met. Anyway, that night he introduced me to your buddy Kevin. All five club owners tell me—despite their drunken, sloppy demeanor—that I should talk to Kevin. "Kevin, talk to this guy. He can help with that problem you told us about with that airline," says Big Joe. So then Kevin introduces himself with his typical salesman smirk.

"So this guy Kevin was great. He overpays in advance and only wants a little crap done. Like for this airline executive, he just wanted me..."

"*Listen Fuck*!" Richard yells. "I don't give a fuck about the airline executive, okay asshole? Just tell me how I got into this fucking mess."

"Okay," Officer Allen agrees. He swallows with another large gulp.

Allen thinks back to a particular morning when he was sitting on his sofa in his boxer shorts watching TV and his cell phone rang.

"So I got a ring on my cell phone one Sunday morning from Kevin, right? He says, 'Hey, buddy, I haven't seen you drinking around the boys lately.' So I told him yeah, that I had been kinda busy with some *real* crime. You know, I joked with him that I have to 'protect and serve.' Kevin then tells me that he's got a guy coming into town the next night and that, if I'm interested, he's got a little job for me. He tells me that it's not as easy as the last job he gave me but that it would be pretty easy. He joked with me that I might even hit my DUI quota for the month.

"So Kevin begins to explain that he is going to take this executive out for a couple of drinks around ten p.m. and then that one of the executives is going to leave later driving a rental vehicle. He tells me to make sure I find a way to stop the guy and test him for a DUI and then make sure, like I did with the other guy, that the executive doesn't pass the test."

"AND," Richard growls.

"AND, AND it got all fucked up. I missed you leaving the damn club and got stuck at the friggin' train tracks."

"I was sitting in my police car banging my hands on the steering wheel yelling," "*Shit*!"

"I turned on my computer and video called Kevin, who was God knows where sounding like he was having a little bit of fun with one of his bitches, as usual. Kevin has his pants down between his ankles thrusting what appears to be some girl on all fours, but you can barely see her around Kevin cause he turns right to pickup his cellphone out of his pants pocket behind him. Without sound Kevin mouths the words "*What*, Fuck I will handle it. Get to the cross street. He will be there."

Now Richard thinks back to that night when he answered Kevin's call on his way back to the hotel.

"Hey, you just drove right by me," he remembers Kevin saying.

"That motherfucker bullshitted me about some drunk girl running away from some guy," Richard says. "I knew that story sounded like bullshit. *Fuck*." Richard hits Officer Allen with the side of his gun, knocking him unconscious. Then he quickly releases Allen's wife and kids, apologizes to his young daughter, and gives her a pat on the head. Richard then races out of the front door of Allen's house to his vehicle that is parked on the street. He jumps in and flips on the radio. Blasting through the speakers for the next thirty minutes is heavy metal music. With each song that plays Rich gets increasingly angry clutching the steering wheel with his sweaty hands causing the leather on the wheel to twist.

Richard jumps out of his car. He approaches a house, sweating and fuming with anger. He knocks on the door. Kevin's voice says, "Who is it?"

With a soft, low-pitched voice, Richard pretends to act defeated, like he needs help. "Kevin, buddy, it's your old friend Rich."

"*Oh*, Rich, shit, it's been a while. How are you doing?" Kevin asks as he unlocks his front door and begins to open it.

Boom! Richard kicks the large front door into Kevin's head. Kevin in his dark blue fleece bathrobe goes flying backward with his robe opening up just enough to notice that it was all he was wearing, as he was obviously not expecting the intrusion. Richard then pounces on him, punching him several times in the face and yelling, "How could you, you fuck? How could you? I had a life. I had a wife, kids. You little motherfucker." Richard continues to punch Kevin in the face and head until his own hands begin to bleed.

The house is a large two-story in the city of Roseville with the typical Palm Springs huge wooden double front doors that look custom built. There is a scream upstairs as a beautiful blond woman who looks a little coked out and is wearing nothing but Kevin's blue dress shirt stands looking down over the wrought iron railing that overlooks the foyer at Richard, who is still repeatedly punching Kevin while sitting on him. Richard doesn't even look up to give her a glimpse; he just focuses on taking his rage and anger out on Kevin. She turns and trips over her own two feet, slightly banging her body and sliding against the wall as she runs back into Kevin's bedroom.

Downstairs, Kevin, after receiving a few blows to the head, grabs and holds onto Richard, enabling him to throw another punch. Richard, who has been up all night with the Allens and is now fighting with Kevin at three in the morning, is physically exhausted. Kevin is finally able to push Richard down off his body toward his feet and land a strong head-butt to him, causing a huge gash above Richard's right eye. Blood and sweat pour from Richard's face into his eye, blinding him.

"Ouch, fuck," Richard yells out.

In the distance, the woman upstairs is on the phone saying, "Hello, police, yeah, a man...." Her voice trails off.

"So, bitch, you figured it out," Kevin mutters. "Dude, I can honestly say I didn't expect it to go down like this at all."

Kevin puts Richard in a chokehold, his mouth up against Richard's ear.

"But really, I just wanted to land that Honda deal myself," he tells Richard. "I'm the one who has been out here kissing these fucking guys' asses for a year. But do I get the big pitch? No. Send party boy Kevin to take the boys out to the strip club. Send party boy Kevin to take the guys out to the bar all night. Send party boy Kevin to get hookers for the executives. Send party boy Kevin to get whatever people fucking want. But never give him a shot to be the man. All around the advertising community I'm known for being the party boy and just a joke." Kevin, holding onto Richard, thinks back in his mind and explains when he got a phone call one day to come down to Miami to the Smothers's corporate office. Betty sounded really excited for him and couldn't wait to see him. It had been about two years since Kevin went down to Miami, and the last time he was down was to celebrate the Exclusive International Hotel chain deal that Richard landed. What a party that was. Betty and Kevin got so drunk at the grand opening of their newest hotel. Kevin slipped away during all the excitement with Betty to go up to her room, but in the elevator Betty unzipped Kevin's pants and preceded to touch his bare penis. Kevin, turned on, made his move. He turned Betty around against the mirrored elevator, hiked up her cock-tail dress, and jammed his two fingers into her stockings near her butt, ripping a hole big enough to fit his entire hand in. Pulling down with force, he ripped the stocking down to her knees and thrusted her right in the elevator.

Two years later, Kevin stood in Mr. Smothers's office, with Betty sitting at the mahogany table with a huge grin in her face while they wait for Mr. Smothers to finish up his phone call. "Okay, great. Now get down here boy," Mr. Smothers says to the person on the other end of the line as he slams the phone down. Mr. Smothers then looks up from his desk with a little smile. "Kevin, I got a job for you boy." Kevin glances over his shoulder to look at Betty, who is smiling ear from ear. "Kevin, you worked for me a long time now." Kevin thinks *Finally! I'm going to get my chance.*

"Oh, good you're finally down here," says Mr. Smothers as he looks behind Kevin. "Look Kevin, take the new guy Pierce through the building and introduce him to everyone. Listen, don't forget to swing by Park's office to see if he needs anything while Pierce is out in California with you next week working on the airline deal. Park can help. Pierce, Betty will book your flight information when you get done with Kevin." Kevin, in shock with a defeated look on his face, walks out with Pierce, and, in the corner of his eye, he sees Betty just as sad.

Barely breathing Richard says, "Well, boo fucking hoo, man."

Kevin releases one hand while the other still holds Richard's throat; he punches Richard in the face from behind.

"So, Rich, my man, it was time to get a chance to get the big job, and I did, didn't I? Just like I landed that airline deal from that rookie Pierce," Kevin says sarcastically.

"You know how old man Smothers is a hug homophobe, I nailed pictures of Pierce and the head airline executive getting a blowjob and a lot more from a transvestite hooker in Pierce's hotel room our first night out on the town in Cali. After I bailed him out of jail he quit the next day with a little encouragement before even moving out here," says Kevin.

Richard, who is still having a tough time breathing, says, "Well I hope you're proud of yourself. It only took you ten years to destroy my life just to get my job, dick."

"Hey, listen. It should have happened three years ago," Kevin mutters up against Richard's ear, spraying him with saliva as he speaks. Then, ever so softly, Kevin says with a whisper, "Yeah, when I fucked your wife"

Richard tries to jerk his body free as Kevin continues.

"Yeah, buddy, she said it was the best sex she had ever had and that she was going to leave you for me. But she felt bad for the children and decided to give it one more chance. I thought for sure that her bouncing on your ass would fuck you up so much to get you kicked out of Smothers for good. No worries, though. I bided my time and look how it paid off. I know once I move into your office in Miami she drop that trainer and come running into my arms," Kevin said, laughing.

"*Motherfucker*," Richard yells. He steps to the side just a little and swings his elbow back right into Kevin's stomach. Then, he swings his arm and uses the back of his fist to hit Kevin right in his ball sack.

Kevin immediately releases his hold on Richard and steps backward, only to trip and fall on the foyer step just beyond the front door.

Kevin lies on the hard tile just inside the wide-open front door. Flashing police lights are everywhere. Richard, now on one knee, is gasping for air and holding his throat, choking. Finally, after a good minute of Richard choking and Kevin groaning as he holds on to his ball sack with both of his hands, they both hear the sound of a rustling stampede coming up the grass in Kevin's yard.

"Hold it right there you two. Let me see both your hands right now," yells an officer.

Richard looks up to the front door. Behind Kevin are four police officers in uniform with guns drawn at both of them. Richard drops to his other knee and raises both hands, still choking and gasping for breath. Two of the officers roll Kevin over, prying his hands away from his balls and cuffing them behind his back. Both Kevin, who is still in his robe, and Richard, who is bleeding and sweating, are cuffed and walked to the waiting police cars on the street. On either side of Kevin's yard, about twenty neighbors look on to see what is happening. They stare at Richard and Kevin, who are looking back at them. Kevin, with his head down, and Richard, with a little grin on his face, are slowly loaded into the police cars. Richard glances to his right at Kevin and says, "This isn't over."

CHAPTER TEN

"LET'S GO," a loud voice says. "You posted bail." The sound of footsteps is heard as the jail cell door shuts.

The light is bright ahead, and an officer sitting behind a mesh opening says, "Here are your belongings."

"Thank you," the man says. His bruised hand opens the door to enter the police station lobby.

With the door half shut, the man asks the officer, "Wait, who bailed me out?"

"It was me, Rich," the blond woman says as Richard turns his head. It was Kevin's girl from his house. "I knew Kevin was bad news, but I had no idea how bad he was," she says. "Rich, I'm sorry about what happened to you."

Richard, exhausted with his head bowed low and a bandage above his eyebrow, starts to walk away when the woman says, "Rich, listen. They dropped all the charges."

With a whisper, she walks up and speaks into Richard's ear. "They never found the gun."

Richard, who can barely move, looks over, says "Thanks," and slowly walks away. Behind him over his shoulder, Richard hears a deputy say, "Mrs. Collin, here is your receipt."

Richard stops turns around and says, "Mrs. Dick Collin?" Richard thinks to himself that Kevin must have planned on using Dick Collin from American Honda's wife to help land the deal. Mrs. Collin looks at Rich raises her index finger to her lips and says, "Shhh."

TEN MONTHS LATER

A RADIO news station reports: "Eighteen months after the Great Recession, economists say the country is on the rise. In other news, Hyundai Motors USA announced today that on Monday they will announce a new senior vice president for marking at their Design and Research Center in California."

The slight roar of an engine shifting into gear can be heard on the long and winding road ahead. It's bright outside with the sun shining. Up ahead in the distance, a car is driving forward; it's getting closer and closer with each second, and the roar of the engine gets louder and louder. A sparkling metallic blue car approaches in the distance. The car approaches fast, and the engine gets louder with every passing second.

Finally, the big-winged badge is seen on the hood as the vehicle comes roaring over a slight hill. Now in full view, the vehicle looks like a Bentley, though it's not. It appears that a man is driving, but his identity is unknown. As a light shines into the side of the vehicle that has all four windows down, the sound of classical music can be heard very softly. The music gets louder to the point that it overpowers the sound of the roaring engine. The driver is still unknown. Then suddenly an arm covered with a dark blue long-sleeve dress shirt appears through the sunroof; the other arm appears to be holding the steering wheel. The music plays still louder, and the man raises his head and looks up through the sunroof. It's Richard.

"I can't stand losing," Richard says, that sexy grin on his face.

There is a slight banging sound that appears to get louder and louder. A slightly muffled sound can be heard also. Both sounds seem to be coming from the trunk of the car. The banging sounds like kicking, and the muffled noise sounds like someone yelling.

A man in a business suit is tied and gagged. As the man struggles to escape, kicking and jerking his body from left to right, he looks up. The man is Kevin, with blood and sweat coming down his face and a handkerchief in his mouth.

The engine roars and the music begins blasting again. The four-door vehicle speeds by. The Hyundai badge is seen and the model name Genesis is visible in the rear. Below is the California license plate with the words "Manufacturer" under the plate number.

ABOUT THE AUTHOR

RALPH H. Perkins has worked in the automotive business for fifteen years, building his expertise in auto sales and marketing. Starting in the automotive business while on a short break from college, He was working 60-70 hours a week at a Toyota Dealership in Fort Lauderdale, Florida. With no intention of making a career out of the automotive business, Ralph received a promotion to become an assistant manager of pilot program joint with east coast Toyota distributor called a Business Development Center.

Perkins success within the local Toyota dealership with digital marketing catapulted his career to some of the largest national automotive companies in the U.S allowing him the autonomy to change focus to advertising and marketing as a fulltime career.

Ralph H. Perkins currently serves as Vice President of Sales & Marketing in one of the top twenty automotive dealer group's in the nation, with more than fifty dealership rooftop franchises over six states, including Florida and California. He found inspiration to begin originally drafting Treatment as a screenplay during long business flights leaving from Miami to and from California. More information can be found at www.ralphHperkins.com

Book Teaser

Up-and-coming advertising executive Richard Park takes a business trip during the 2008-2009 economic recession. What should be a short lark in California to mix business with pleasure turns into a nightmare that upends his stable life. While in California, Richard is stalled by a routine traffic stop. But instead of being routinely processed by the courts, Richard finds his professional and personal life thrown into an unending downward spiral.

But when Richard finds himself at the end of his rope, he will be forced to take justice into his own hands. This fast-paced novel of greed, politics, and corruption by Ralph H. Perkins, IV starts from the climactic ending and works backwards through flashbacks to reveal the sordid problems of Richard's life. Eventually, readers begin to feel compassion and empathy for the chain of corrupt events and ruthless free market tactics that have made his life so difficult.

As an upper-middle-class member hit hard by government regulation, Richard seems to embody the tens of thousands of professionals knocked down by the recession. Yet in this audacious thriller of underperforming capitalism and overzealous government, Richard will become the victim of a conspiracy built on robbing the livelihoods of hard-working Americans.

Perkins has worked in the automotive business for fifteen years, overseeing fifty dealerships in six states. He was inspired to write *Treatment* on long business flights to and from California. More information can be found at www.ralphHperkins.com